Samuel French Acting Edition

Lucifer's Child

A One-Woman Play by
William Luce

Based on the writings of
Isak Dinesen

SAMUELFRENCH.COM   SAMUELFRENCH.CO.UK

MUSIC USE NOTE

Licensees are solely responsible for obtaining formal written permission from copyright owners to use copyrighted music in the performance of this play and are strongly cautioned to do so. If no such permission is obtained by the licensee, then the licensee must use only original music that the licensee owns and controls. Licensees are solely responsible and liable for all music clearances and shall indemnify the copyright owners of the play(s) and their licensing agent, Samuel French, against any costs, expenses, losses and liabilities arising from the use of music by licensees. Please contact the appropriate music licensing authority in your territory for the rights to any incidental music.

IMPORTANT BILLING AND CREDIT REQUIREMENTS

If you have obtained performance rights to this title, please refer to your licensing agreement for important billing and credit requirements.

ACKNOWLEDGEMENTS

The author wishes to thank Florence Feiler and Clara Selborn with Rungstedlund Foundation for the rights to Isak Dinesen's *Out of Africa*, *Shadows on the Grass* and *Letters From Africa*. Thanks are also extended to poet Eugene Walter for the use of lines from his *Monkey Poems*, biographer Judith Thurman, researcher Janet Jurist, Charles Nelson Reilly and translator Grant Michael Menzies. An excerpt from Rupert Brooke is quoted. Cover photograph of Julie Harris by Bill Crockett. *Brown Eyes, Why Are You Blue?* copyright 1925 Mills Music, Inc. Renewed 1958 Mills Music, Inc. and Fred Fisher Music Co. Inc. Lyrics by Al Bryan, music by George W. Meyer. All rights reserved. Used by permission.

Note: Isak Dinesen's illustration for the story of the stork may be found in *Out of Africa*. The original incidental music composed for the Broadway production is not available. Producers are free to develop their own sound cues. The Danish lullaby used in Act II can be found at the back of this book. Permission to perform *Brown Eyes, Why Are You Blue?* may be obtained from EMI Music Publishing, 810 Seventh Avenue, 36th floor, New York, NY 10019, Attention: Stage Licensing.

ABOUT ISAK DINESEN

When the elderly Isak Dinesen came to New York in 1959 to tell her stories to charmed audiences, I knew little about her. It was not until 1960 that I became acquainted with the writings of this great storyteller. A friend, Kimmis Hendrick, presented me with his worn copy of Dinesen's *Seven Gothic Tales*. Beguiled by the baroque exoticism and dreamlike atmosphere of the stories, I immediately tried to obtain Dinesen's second book, the ravishing *Out of Africa*. After unsuccessfully calling three libraries and several bookstores, I secured a first edition from a rare book dealer. I treasure that first edition, as I do the earlier gift of *Tales* from my friend. Today there are probably few bookstores or libraries which do not carry the timeless, imaginative stories of this brilliant Danish writer. Her tales have been translated into many languages. They are now in popular paperback editions. Two major Academy Award motion pictures, *Out of Africa* and *Babette's Feast,* have most recently increased Isak Dinesen's audience by many millions. Other films are forthcoming. Born Karen Christentze Dinesen on April 17, 1885, Isak Dinesen was raised in an upperclass Victorian family in Rungstedlund, Denmark. Late in 1913, at the age of 28, Karen sailed to Mombasa, where she married her cousin, Baron Bror von Blixen-Finecke. They settled on a large plantation in the highlands of Kenya and set about raising coffee. She became friend and physician to the natives there. But after a few years her marriage to Bror Blixen disintegrated, ending in divorce. In spite of the divorce, Karen remained in Kenya, not only because of her consuming love for one man, the high-born Englishman Denys Finch Hatton, but also because she still hoped to make a success of the coffee plantation. But the land was too high for coffee and it was hard work to keep it going. What was hard work in the beginning became fruitless toil in the end. In 1931 the coffee market collapsed. Then Finch Hatton died in a plane crash. Baroness Blixen returned to her ancestral home in Denmark, bankrupt, bereaved and temporarily defeated, but with aspirations for becoming a writer. For the rest of her life Karen would prefer to be called Baroness, though she adopted Isak Dinesen as her literary name. Her first book was *Seven Gothic Tales,* published in 1934. With the eye of a realist and the soul of a sorceress, she crafted these elegant, seductive, fantastic tales in the style of the ancient soothsayers. "The divine art is the story," she said. "In the beginning was the story." Hers was the primitive art of storytelling that harked back to ancient oral tradition. *Out of Africa* followed in 1937. Her subsequent works were *Winter's Tales* in 1942, *Last Tales* in 1957, *Anecdotes of Destiny* in 1958, *Shadows on the Grass* in 1960 and *Ehrengard* in 1963. Karen lived out her years at Rungstedlund, as ill health gradually took its toll—a result of having contracted syphilis from her husband during their first year of marriage. With the Faustian rationale of a true mystic, she justified what to most women would have been a tragic plight. She called herself "Lucifer's Child," claiming to have sold her soul to the rebellious, light-bearing Archangel and receiving in exchange a gift of tales which the whole world would read. "I am the child of Lucifer," she wrote to her brother Thomas in 1926, "and the angel's song is not for me." As if by some secret, compassionate Providence, Karen devised this allegorical argument for the plight in which she found herself. She described herself as being caught "in a pit, in a dark place." She wanted out of the dark place all of her life. Her favorite Bible passage was, "I will not let thee go, except thou bless me" - Jacob's passionate bargain as he struggled with the angel at Peniel. The angel's blessing for Jacob was redemption and the new name, Israel. In her own Peniel experience, Baroness Karen Blixen wrestled with her dark angel and exacted a similar redemption. She became Isak Dinesen, the light-bearing storyteller of the century.

William Luce

THE MUSIC BOX

THE ESTATE OF IRVING BERLIN AND THE SHUBERT ORGANIZATION, OWNERS

RONALD S. LEE

presents

JULIE HARRIS

in

LUCIFER'S CHILD

a new play by

WILLIAM LUCE

based on the writings of Isak Dinesen

Incidental Music by **CHARLES GROSS**

Scenery	Costumes	Lighting
MARJORIE BRADLEY KELLOGG	**NOEL TAYLOR**	**PAT COLLINS**

Sound by **T. RICHARD FITZGERALD**

Directed by

TONY ABATEMARCO

LUCIFER'S CHILD was developed and first performed at Duke University, going on to Kennedy Center and Boston before its Broadway opening on April 4, 1991. Julie Harris received a Tony nomination as Best Actress.

CHARACTER

Isak Dinesen, Baroness Karen Blixen

PLACE

Karen Blixen's study at Rungstedlund, Denmark

TIME

Act I: New Year's Eve, 1958

Act II: April, 1959

LUCIFER'S CHILD

ACT I

SETTING: Karen Blixen's study at Rungstedlund, Denmark, is furnished with a desk and chair, a two-door armoire with mirrors inside both doors, a small table and shelves filled with books. Upstage, we see a dining room area with a table and chairs. A door leads out to a veranda. Danish china and Karen's African paintings adorn a high shelf above the portal. There are exotic, colorful artifacts from Africa about. At stage right stands a painted Chinese screen. Before it are a large African-type jardiniere, a burnished chest, and large floor cushions covered in African fabrics. Tall spears stand inside the jardiniere. Near center stage is Karen's desk, on which sits her old Corona typewriter. In a green leather frame on the desk is a photograph of Denys Finch Hatton, with other framed photographs of Karen and family; also pictures of Karen and Bror Blixen in Africa and a champagne glass. Beside the desk are a waste basket, a typewriter case and an ice bucket containing a bottle of champagne. In large porcelain vases are dried flowers. A cuckoo clock and a rifle are mounted on a wall. Beside the armoire at stage left are a lamp table and more floor cushions covered in beautiful African fabrics. On the bottom shelf of the table is a

*chamber pot. At far stage left, a gramophone with
records sits on the floor.*

*AT RISE: We see Isak Dinesen's rooms at Rungstedlund,
Denmark, on New Year's Eve, 1958. The
GRAMOPHONE is playing, "Brown Eyes, Why Are
You Blue?" We see suitcases and hat boxes at stage
right, where a trunk is open. The room is chaotic.
Gowns, hats and furs are draped about, waiting to be
packed. At stage left hang more clothes, and in the
armoire are clothes as yet unselected. KAREN BLIXEN
(ISAK DINESEN), seventy-three, appears onstage in a
wilted satin Pierrot costume and plumed hat. SHE is
frail and unsteady. SHE carries a pair of shoes in each
hand.*

KAREN. (*To audience.*) I don't know where I'll pack
these. I'm already taking seven pairs. But I may need them
in New York. And I'll be in Boston six days.

*(SHE wedges the shoes into the open trunk, singing along
with the record.)*

RECORDED VOICE & KAREN.
Brown eyes, why are you blue?
Brown eyes, what can I do?

KAREN. (*To audience.*) The airlines are so finicky
about excess weight. It's not like the old days, when we
traveled with trunks. (*SHE has moved to stage left, where
SHE removes the needle from the record and turns off the*

machine.) I had nine black enameled iron trunks when I sailed to Africa in 1913. Uncle Aage bought them for me as a wedding present. They had brass Excelsior locks and leather handles. (*SHE opens the armoire door and takes out a mandolin. SHE limps painfully downstage. Her emaciated look is heightened by white makeup and eyes heavily lined with kohl.*) Well? What do you think? The costume, I mean—for a masquerade ball. Who knows? When I go to New York, I may be invited to one. Aunt Lidda made it for me when I was thirteen. It still fits. I wore it for a family theatrical that I wrote. "Harlequin's Folly," I called it. My sisters and I performed it. Ea played Columbine, Elle was Harlequin and I played Pierrot.

(*SHE strums the out-of-key strings, then kneels. Tivoli MUSIC underscores. As Pierrot.*)

KAREN.
Fair Columbine!
Voluptuous care, in whom I hope!
Heed not the blandishments of Harlequin,
But list unto the song I sing,
Embrace the tribute which I bring,
Of lilies white and roses red.
O Columbine,
Be mine!
    (*Standing again. To audience.*) The costume was a splendid success. Well, the tulle ruff is lovely. I wore it again last September in Copenhagen at a party for the Heretica writers' group, and it fell flat. I don't know why. It looks the same as it did sixty-one years ago. (*SHE puts*

away the mandolin, then removes two capes from the armoire.) But there's no room in my luggage. Besides, the Ford Foundation has filled my agenda with press conferences and interviews for Random House. No, there'll be no masquerade ball. Anyway, tonight would have been the night for Pierrot's New York début. It's New Year's Eve. Tomorrow is January first, 1959.

On January second I'm leaving for New York, where I'll tell my stories. My secretary-companion, Clara Svendsen, will go with me—my Sancho Panza. Also, Cousin Tove will tag along. Tove is my age. She's a good sort, blunt and earthy. And she carries her weight so well. (*To Clara, calling.*) Clara! Did Tove say she wanted to borrow the burgundy cape or the peacock? (*SHE drops the peacock cape on the cushions. To herself.*) But the burgundy's too small for Tove. (*To audience.*) I give names to all my outfits. This is called Cape of Good Hope. When I named it, I didn't know Tove would be wearing it. (*SHE drops the burgundy cape on the chest at stage right. A suit.*) Over here is Black Grouse. (*A dress.*) Petit Diable. (*Evening gowns.*) Sappho, with sequins. The plunging neckline is Tate Gallery. Hortense. I don't remember why I named this Hortense. (*A suit.*) And this is my favorite. Sober Truth. (*SHE appraises her Pierrot costume in the mirror once more. To herself.*) It does look a bit crushed. Perhaps a little freshening with the iron. Aunt Lidda would be happy to know I still have it. (*SHE hangs Hortense in the armoire, then removes her Pierrot hat. Her hair is gray. SHE sits on the edge of the armoire shelf. To audience.*) Auntie lived to be very old. Her whole world was the geese she tended every day. They were her brood of children. After the war, she was deathly afraid the communists would take over Denmark and kill the geese. (*To Aunt Lidda.*) No, no, Auntie, the commissars will give you a limousine and driver and send you all over the country inspecting geese. Your title will be "Comrade Goose Lady of the People's Republic of Denmark." (*Standing. To audience.*) I believe a woman's clothes are an extension of her inner being. Perhaps I value clothes too highly. Let me see, what was the first garment I ever gave a name to? Was it the pinafore? (*SHE removes the Pierrot ruff. To Clara.*) Clara! What did I call the blue pinafore? The one in the picture? I told you once. Now I've forgotten. (*To audience.*) Rapunzel. Yes, that sounds right. I think it was Rapunzel. (*Another dress.*) I'll appear in Boston and Washington, as well as in New York City. A keynote speaker, they call me. But I'll only tell my stories. A storyteller is what I am, a member of an ancient, idle, wild and useless tribe. (A suit.) Marlene. (*SHE takes Marlene to stage right and hangs it with the other clothes.*) As a child, I kept my sister Elle awake at night by telling stories. (*To Elle, whispering.*) Elle? Elle? (*To audience.*) "Oh, Karen," she'd say, "you're always telling, telling, telling. I'd like to sleep a little, if you don't mind." But I couldn't help myself. The stories have always been there. Prick me with a pin and out they flow.

I go by several names. Karen Christentze Dinesen is the name I was born with, though most call me Tanne. Father called me Ta-Ta. The Danes call me Baroness. For a good many years, I was Baroness von Blixen-Finecke. But my literary name is Isak Dinesen. I always wanted to be a man. Do you like "Isak?" It means "the one who laughs." Tove says it's misleading. I don't know what she's talking about. (*SHE pauses and surveys the room.*) In this room—long ago—I packed my trousseau, to set sail for Africa. I have sometimes thought of going back there, but, no, I would feel like a ghost. I am too far removed in space and time from that eager, foolish young woman who set her heart on Africa.

(*SHE dons the cape and walks downstage, as if stepping outside. Light change to MOONLIGHT.*)

KAREN. It is my final dream to fly to America. Other dreams have come to nought: to become a great chef in Paris, to make a pilgrimage to Mecca, to start a hospital in Nairobi for Masai children—Dr. Schweitzer talked me out of that one. Now I feel a mysterious emotion, an old excitement, to be packing again—this time for America.

Today Dr. Ziersen said, "Don't go to America, Baroness. You are too ill and could die there." (*To Dr. Ziersen.*) Doctor Ziersen, I'm three thousand years old. I have dined with Socrates. No! I have set my heart on America. I will not die there.

(*To audience.*) The trouble is, I'm on the verge of what is generally known as "going to the dogs." Soon it will be too late to go anywhere else. A fatalism pursues me, sometimes demonic. I *must* get to America before I am overtaken.

I see Orion the Hunter is tracking the stars as usual. And is that Venus? My darling brother Thomas would know. "The bright and morning star," Tommy calls it—after Revelation. Yesterday, Clara asked me why I step out here every night, then go to my room and shut the door. (*As Clara.*) You've been doing it for years, Tanne. What does it signify? (*To Clara.*) I'm looking southeast toward Africa, Clara, where half of me lies in the Ngong Hills. (*To Denys.*) Goodnight, Denys.

(*Walking back to the   room and discarding the cape. LIGHT returns to normal.*)

KAREN. (*To audience.*) And when I come in here and shut the door, it is to look at the map of my farm in Kenya ... (*Picking up Denys's picture.*) ... and to touch this. My friend, Denys Finch Hatton. The Honorable Denys Finch Hatton. Denys called me Tania. I am so fortunate to have realized my ideal in him. It is exactly forty-one years ago that I walked into Muthaiga Club in Nairobi and came face-to-face for the first time with this extraordinary hunter. That such a beautiful man existed, I had never dared believe. (*SHE packs Denys's picture. To audience member.*) Is it possible, I wonder, for a woman to live on passion alone? Or would it burn out your heart in time? Does anyone know? (*Gazing in mirror.*) Do you?

(*Tivoli MUSIC.*)

KAREN.
O foolish Pierrot,
If love burned your lips
Like some bold coquette,
Would you pirouette?
Dance a menuet?

Sing a chansonnette?
(*Singing.*) Plaisir d'amour
Ne dure quand moment.

(*MUSIC out. SHE pulls out another gown from the armoire.*)

KAREN.   When I'm in New York, I'm going to Harlem to hear jazz. I also want to meet the film actress, Marilyn Monroe. After my commitment to the Foundation is fulfilled, I'd like to go to the state called Wisconsin to look for my father's cabin. Frydenlund, he named it. Happy Grove. (*SHE unfolds a large map on the desk.*) As a young man, Father sailed to North America. I found his old map this morning, and traced his journey all the way to that village with the exotic name. What was it? (*Finding it on map.*) Oshkosh! Father's cabin was near Oshkosh, on a bluff where Wolf River and Swamp Creek meet. He lived by a Chippewa encampment, which explains why there are a good many blue-eyed Chippewa. He fished and trapped and shot ducks. He even baked his own bread. My father could do anything.

Aunt Christentze maintained that Father fled to America in grief over the death of his beautiful cousin Agnes Frijs. Auntie believed that when Father committed suicide twenty-five years later, it was still over Agnes. I know why Father hanged himself from the rafters, though I never speak of it. (*SHE looks closely at a gown, then opens the other armoire door. Inside is a chart with the names of her outfits. SHE checks the columns.*) Beau Brummel, Beau Brummel—ah. No, I don't think I'll take it with me. Very chic, but it says here—I've been photographed in it twice. *(SHE sits on the pillows, removing and folding the Pierrot pants. SHE wears slacks underneath.)* Many years ago, when I lived on my farm in Africa, I generally wore old khaki slacks stained with oil, mud and fouling. Once—wearing these old clothes—I wore my pearl earrings as well. I looked so unfeminine, that a Kikuyu referred to me as "that small bwana with white stones in his ears."

When Edward, Prince of Wales—the future king of England—came to Nairobi for a visit, I hadn't been to Europe for four years and had no idea what the fashions were. So I wrote Pacquin's in Paris, which had my measurements, and asked them to make me a gown in silver brocade with a hooped skirt of great fullness. I called it Coronation.

(SHE stands. Rhythmic, percussive SOUNDS of Africa fade in.)

KAREN. The fateful Friday arrived, November 28, 1928, and the Prince came to dine with me at the farm. Afterwards, a big Ngoma was held, the ritual dance of harvest. That night there were three thousand natives by my house. The moon was full. There was no breath of wind. A great ring of naked dancers jumped up and down, heads thrown back, feet stamping the ground. With swinging of spears, with deadly, monotonous pulse—their red-chalked faces took on an expression of angelic ecstasy. It was a fine Ngoma. I have seen no finer anywhere.

(SOUNDS OUT.)

KAREN. Afterward, the Kikuyu elders came to see me. The chief was their spokesman—my friend Kinanjui—a courtly old man in a cape of blue monkey skins. (*As Kikuyu Chief.*) Msabu, we think that on the night when the Toto a Soldani came here to see our young men and virgins dance, among the Msabus present you had on the nicest frock. It pleased our hearts, Msabu. For we all believe that every day on the farm, you are terribly badly dressed. (*Another gown.*) Boheme. It's never been worn. I've been saving it several years for a certain prestigious event in Stockholm. But it hasn't left the closet yet, and now I don't think it ever will. When Mr. Ernest Hemingway accepted his Nobel Prize, he told the judges, "Isak Dinesen should have been considered before me." I'm sure they didn't appreciate his advice. (*SHE finds a gold turban and puts it on.*) Halo. I'm excited to be journeying to America for the first time. My earliest motto in life was, "Navigare necesse est vivere non necesse"—to set sail somewhere is more important than life itself. So I'm setting sail again. (*Sitting in armoire again.*) Of course, I'll miss Rungstedlund, but it's only for three months. Everything here gathers itself around me, and from day to day I feel as if my mother were sharing in every part of my life. Last night I dreamed about her again, the same dream. I am running on the path through the glade, and when I emerge from the trees, I see her—(*Moved.*) No. I cannot speak of it. To return to your mother and feel her arms around you is a dream that haunts you till you die. (*SHE opens a drawer in the armoire.*) I mustn't forget my fascinator. It's snowing in New York. (*SHE pulls out a dark woolen scarf.*) Oh, and my scarf. (*Draping it about her neck.*) It seems to get longer every year. (*SHE uncovers a shawl and takes it out.*) And my Somali shawl which I brought back from Africa. (*Back to the scarf.*) Aunt Bess knit this for me during the German occupation. It was three and a half feet long and extravagantly wide. Now it's six feet long and extravagantly narrow. (*Putting scarf around neck.*) Aunt Bess and my mother, Ingeborg, were sisters. Aunt Bess was one year younger, and the true matriarch of our family. Mary Bess Westenholz. (*SHE pulls out an album and displays a picture of Aunt Bess.*) She never married. She moved here three years before I was born and stayed for sixty years. Every inch a conservative, militant Unitarian and outspoken suffragette. "Tanne," she once barked at me, "you're entirely too frivolous, just like your father's sisters. They're capricious beyond words. Scandinavian girls are in danger of corruption by atheism and free love. And it's all the fault of men. I myself do not hold sacred a pair of stupid trousers. It is my practice never to importune a man for anything, even when I say The Lord's Prayer." (*To Aunt Bess.*) What do you mean, Aunt Bess? (*As Aunt Bess.*) I mean: "You give us our daily bread! You lead us not into temptation! You deliver us from evil!" Always let the man know who's boss. You see? (*Crossing to stage right with shawl. SHE wraps herself in it. To audience.*) The Somalis have such elegant taste. My most trusted servant in Africa was a Somali, and a Mohammedan. His name was Farah Aden. When I think back on the episodes of my life there, his figure, straight, candid, and very fine to look at, stands as doorkeeper to all of them. My husband-to-be sent Farah to meet me in Aden in 1913. I was on my way to Mombasa to marry my cousin, the Swedish Baron Bror von Blixen-Finecke, and live in the highlands of Kenya on a coffee farm of forty-five hundred acres, financed by Mother's family.

For almost eighteen years, Farah ran my house, my stables and safaris. I talked to him about my worries and about my successes, and he knew of all that I did or thought. He was my best friend. (*SHE removes the turban and puts it in a hatbox. Then SHE turns to a photograph on the desk. To audience.*) This shows me all decked out at the castle at Wedellsborg. See the satin gloves? They stretched right up to the armpits. Pelleas and Melisande. Clara calls ... (*SHE pauses and looks offstage. Whispering.*) Clara calls gloves Right and Left, but that's too general. (*SHE crosses and opens the armoire drawer.*) These kid gloves are Tristan and Isolde. And here, these lace ones are Iphigenie and ... oh, you know the opera. Did she have a mate? Or was it her brother? Well, let's call him Max. Iphigenie and Max. (*Crossing, SHE puts the gloves in the trunk.*) Aunt Bess wouldn't have named one solitary thing after a man. She despaired over the men in Parliament, and criticized their indifferent handling of Denmark's defense. In 1909 she made the headlines by marching into the Lower House of Parliament in Session, shoving the doorman aside and seizing the bell from the chairman.

(*LIGHT change. SHE picks up a bell from the desk and furiously rings it.*)

KAREN. (*As Aunt Bess.*) You Danish men are nothing but pompous old fools! You sit here bartering away the welfare of our country! Well, I'm here to tell you that the women of Denmark despise you and brand you as a bunch of lazy, loud-mouthed, do-nothing politicians who've betrayed the honor of your country!

(*LIGHT back to normal.*)

KAREN. (*To audience.*) The members were paralyzed. Not a word was spoken, except for the chairman, Anders Thomsen, who kept babbling, "She took my bell!" Anders never did get it back. Aunt Bess carried it home, and was too embarrassed to return it. (*SHE rings bell vigorously, then silences it suddenly. To Clara.*) Oh, yes, Clara, I'm all right. I was just practicing for the New Year. (*SHE exchanges the turban for a large hat with swooping feathers.*) Albatross. (*As if at court.*) Queen Victoria, I presume? The name is Baroness von Blixen-Finecke. Your Highness. (*A curtsy. To audience.*) I admit, I'm one of God's chosen snobs. Unfortunately, my husband, the Baron, was not. (*SHE painfully straightens up from the curtsy. SHE winces and touches her spine.*) Oh, it's nothing. It will pass.

A year after my arrival in Africa, I learned that Bror was involved with Masai women, which explains why there are a good many blue-eyed Masai. I learned of Bror's philandering too late. The flowering of Nemesis had begun inside me. (*SHE removes the shawl from her shoulders.*) In those days, mercury tablets were worthless. Even Dr. Erlich's magic bullet—salvarsan injections—in my case, turned out to be a blank cartridge. So even though the disease reached a non-communicable stage, I was never cured. I felt as if a claw had grabbed my heart, as if I'd been shaken and tumbled by some wild animal. (*From the armoire, SHE wraps herself in a fox neck-piece and looks in the mirror.*) Beowulf. But the hat's wrong. (*Off with the hat.*) There are two things a woman can do in such a situation. Accept it or shoot the man. I didn't shoot Bror. Instead, I made a pact with Lucifer, God's rebellious lover. So love I God. The echo of God's voice ordering him from Heaven is Lucifer's hope in hell. I gave my soul to Lucifer. In return he promised to transmute my sorrow into tales the whole world would read. So you see, I'm Lucifer's child. And if it didn't sound so beastly, I might say that, the world being what it is, it was worth having syphilis just to be called "Baroness." (*SHE packs the hat in the trunk, drapes the fur over it, then sits on the chest at stage right.*) For a long time, I told the family I had a tropical disease. A good thing, too, with Aunt Bess officiating as the moral conscience of the clan. She disliked Bror from the start. (*SHE lights a cigarette in a holder, using a lighter.*) Granduncle Hansen would also have disliked Bror. Even though he lustily sired several children, he looked upon sexual matters with grim abhorrence. So, as the story goes, when his eldest son was stricken with certain embarrassing symptoms, he was summoned to Granduncle's study. (*As Granduncle.*) Have you been smitten in a loathsome and abominable manner by the unspeakable disease which, if known to decent society, would consign you to the wretched ranks of disgusting untouchables who live in odious shame and degradation and

to whom no honorable person will ever speak again? Well?
(*To audience.*) What my poor cousin had was an ulcer. The
whole family had ulcers. (*SHE checks her watch.*) It will
soon be midnight. There'll be celebrating down on the
beach—young people seeing in the New Year. They shoot
off firecrackers and honk their horns, and one may even fire
a rifle over the Sound in the direction of Sweden.
Sometimes there are fireworks. (*SHE puts out her cigarette
and stands, looking across the stage into the armoire
mirror.*) If only there were room in my luggage.

(*Tivoli MUSIC.*)

KAREN. (*As Pierrot.*)
Glad would I be, O Columbine,
Bright passion of my heart,
That, giving you the stars of heaven,
I might be given in return
A little glance from your imperial eye,
A little touch from your imperial hand,
A little dream before we say goodbye.

(*SHE gathers up the Pierrot hat and ruff and puts them in
the open trunk.*)

KAREN. Pierrot, you heartsick fool, you're going to
America, if I have to pack you under Tove's bloomers.

(*The cuckoo CLOCK sounds the half hour. SHE removes
and folds the Pierrot smock, putting it in the trunk.*

SHE is wearing a long-sleeved silk blouse with high neck.)

KAREN. This old German clock is like the one I had at Mbogani House in Kenya. I sold it when I lost the farm.

In the African Highlands, a clock is entirely an object of luxury. All the year round you can tell time from the position of the sun. But at Mbogani just before the impudent cuckoo flung open its little door to announce the hour in a clear, insolent voice, a wonderful thing happened ... *(Sitting at the desk, SHE finds a small paper bag.)* What's this? *(Dumping out its contents.)* Oh, Clara bought new toiletries for the trip. Glycerin soap, tooth powder, comb, toothbrush—but she got blue. I wanted red.

(SHE tosses the new toothbrush into the waste basket. Delicate MUSIC of Africa fades in. LIGHT change.)

KAREN. Anyway, what happened was—just before the cuckoo appeared, Native children came from everywhere. I could see them approaching the house from all sides, at the tails of their goats, which they dared not leave behind. The heads of the children and of the goats swam through the bush and long grass like heads of frogs in a pond.

They left their flocks on the lawn and came in noiselessly on bare feet. The bigger ones were about ten years and the youngest two. They didn't touch anything, nor sit down, nor speak. As the cuckoo rushed out at them, a movement of ecstasy and suppressed laughter ran through the group.

One small Kikuyu herdboy, Wawerru, would come back in the early morning by himself, stand for a long time in front of the clock and address it in Kikuyu in a slow singsong declaration of love. "Nanini nyoni, nanini nyoni, nanini nyoni."

(MUSIC out. LIGHT to normal.)

KAREN. Farah laughed at him. *(To Farah.)* But, Farah, you've stood and waited for the cuckoo. I've seen you. *(As Farah.)* Memsahib, I watch only ten or four times, maybe none at all. But the Kikuyu they believe the bird is alive. They talk to it. The Kikuyu are a stupid people. Kikuyu cuckoo. *(To Farah.)* Yes, Farah. *(SHE finds a bulky fur coat and puts it on. To audience.)* I'll wear this on the plane. Ursa Minor. Some poor old bear from Finland, I suppose. I wore it in Rome last autumn. Well, as long as I have furs, I must wear them. But I'll never buy another. It seems an arrogant use of animals, and is even—I believe— a kind of cosmic disrespect. *(SHE looks around the room.)* I can't find my beauty box. I know it's here. It has all my new cosmetics. *(Finding them.)* Ah! Right under my nose. *(SHE takes the makeup case to the desk, opens it and puts on a makeup scarf. SHE powders her face.)* I don't approve of modern cosmetics. Too garish. A ghostly pallor is far more chic, a thespian mask of mystery. It gives an ethereal quality to a woman. After Grandmother Westenholz became senile, the color drained from her face so totally—we called her Moonbeam. *(To Grandmother.)* Good morning, Moonbeam, did you eat your prunes like a good girl? *(To audience.)* When Cousin Daisy came for a visit, she tiptoed into her room. "Excuse me, but I'm looking for a Moonbeam."

"Here I am!" shrieked Grandmother. (*Applying lipstick. Singing.*)
Brown eyes, why are you blue?
Brown eyes, what can I do?

(*SHE opens the jar of kohl and applies it to her eyes.*)

KAREN. My Egyptian beauty secrets. The first is white powder. Then dark crimson lipstick. The third is kohl around the eyes. Kohl is far superior to manufactured eye pencils. It's made from an age-old compound called antimony. One day Tove watched me doing this. (*As Tove.*) What's that, Karen? (*To Tove.*) It's called kohl. (*As Tove.*) You mean the stuff they burn in stoves? (*To Tove.*) No, Tove, that's C-O-A-L. This is K-O-H-L. It was used by Cleopatra. It's very exotic. It's made from antimony. Do you know what antimony is? (*As Tove.*) Yes. It's the money men pay their ex-wives. (*SHE finishes her eyes. To audience.*) As for Egyptian beauty secret number four, my lips are sealed. (*Closing case and putting it back.*) I hope Tove's presence on the trip won't prove to be a mistake. She doesn't fool me. She's going for one reason and one reason only—to have a good time. She doesn't give a damn about my stories.

Had I a nephew who was still a child, I'd take him with me. I've always had a predilection for boys. The strong sex reaches its highest point of lovableness at the age of twelve to seventeen not to get it back in a second flowering till the age of seventy to ninety. (*SHE sits on the chest.*)

"Tore," I once said to my brother Tommy's boy, "how would you like me to buy you a tattoo for Christmas?" Every young man should have a tattoo. Naturally, the lad was enthusiastic. That is, until he told his parents. His mother Jonna is quite liberal, but not Tommy. I feel sorry for him. And we used to be so close. When Tommy was thirteen and I was twenty, he was so proud to be able to teach me about astronomy. (*As Thomas.*) Look, Tanne! Capella and Cassiopeia—and that strange star Algol. See how it pulses! (*To audience.*) Tommy introduced me to the sky. I introduced him to Shakespeare and to the temerity of believing in nothing. And to Africa. Tommy came to see me in Kenya twice. The first time for two years. My brother, my friend, my confidante. Now we're at odds with each other about everything. "Tanne," he said, "stop interfering in our children's lives. Tore is not going to be tattooed. Stop filling his head with your impossible ideas."

(*SHE drops off the fur coat, goes to the ice bucket by the desk and pours herself a glass.*)

KAREN. To the New Year, to New York, to new life, to new moons, to new worlds, to new everything. (*Drinking.*) Dr. Ziersen says I'm not to drink any alcoholic beverage. (*As Dr. Ziersen, slowly.*) Baroness, I must insist. It's poison to your delicate system. Abstinence is the watchword. (*To Dr. Ziersen.*) Dr. Ziersen, I can't agree more. Abstinence is a most wise thing ... (*To audience.*) ... when practiced in moderation. I never argue with Dr. Ziersen. It's too arduous. He speaks so slowly, I can't follow him.

Champagne, grapes and oysters. That's my diet.
Strangely, I'm unaffected by champagne. Oh, after several
glasses, perhaps. In Africa, Bror drank a bottle of gin a day
and never showed it. On opening each new bottle, he'd say
with great gravity, "Life is life, and fun is fun, but it's all
so quiet when the goldfish die." (*Crossing to the armoire.*)
What that means is anybody's guess. At the Muthaiga
Club, Bror had everyone believing it was the riddle of the
universe. It sounded so inscrutably wise in the cocktail bar,
where he and his cronies met regularly. "It's all so quiet
when the goldfish die."

Fish-balls. (*SHE takes a leopard hat from the armoire.*)
One of my African trophies. Mosaic. In my Kenya days, I
couldn't wait till I'd killed specimens of the Big Five—
lion, elephant, rhino, Cape buffalo and leopard. One day I
killed forty-four animals with a hundred cartridges. The
Natives called me Lioness Blixen. I look back on the
safaris of my youth, with the dogs and the happy breathless
boys around me, seeing a herd of elephant pacing as if they
had an appointment at the end of the world. I wish I could
relive safari with Bror, but without carnage. (*Putting hat
back, SHE sits in the armoire and takes up the album
again.*) There's a picture of Bror with me in here—in
1914—with two lions we shot. I remember thrusting this
in his face and saying, "Bror, I'm no longer this person.
I've changed. Why haven't you?" (*As Bror.*) Why should I
change? Hunting is my life. (*To Bror.*) But you're
poaching ivory to pay off drinking debts, and leaving the
carcasses to rot. (*As Bror.*) Oh, stop preaching. You're
worse than Aunt Bess. No wonder the women here don't
like you. The Commissioner's wife thinks you're a queer

duck, and Lady Delamere says you're a cold fish." (*To Bror,
pretended lament.*) A queer duck and a cold fish. Oh,
merciful saviour, I'm ostracized from the social affairs of a
town that resembles an empty anchovy tin. (*Standing,
SHE takes out Hortense and poses with it before the
mirror. To audience.*) Next to Lady Delamere, I suppose I
was a cold fish. (*To herself.*) Maybe I *will* need this. (*To
audience.*) When the Prince of Wales was honored at
Muthaiga, Gladys Delamere bombarded him across the
table with slices of French bread. Then she climbed over
the Beef Wellington, slipped in the aspic, fell into his lap,
overturned his chair, and the two of them went sprawling
on the floor. After that drunken exhibition, her ladyship
threw up in the foyer and passed out. It took four men to
carry her out. And what was Bror's observation of the
episode? (*As Bror.*) Good old Gladys! Now there's a woman
among women. (*To audience.*) Well, what can you expect
from a man who doesn't know if the French Revolution
came before or after the Crusades? (*SHE puts the dress back
in the armoire, then moves toward the desk.*) No, I don't
think so. (*Pause.*) Our divorce was final in 1925. For some
perverse reason, I derive amusement from the knowledge
that Bror's second wife was a notoriously bad shot. Cockie
Birkbeck. When she married Bror, she became Baroness
Cockie Birkbeck Blixen. After divorcing him, she refused
to surrender her title. So when she married Jan Hoogterp,
she called herself Baroness Cockie Birkbeck Blixen
Hoogterp—not what you would call a musical name, by
any means.

I never met Bror's third wife, Eva Dixon, who, upon
marrying him, became Baroness Eva Dixon Blixen. So

now there were three Baronesses von Blixen, because I also
refused to surrender the title. When Eva died in a car crash
in India, Cockie was living in South Africa. The
Johannesburg newspaper mistakenly reported Cockie's
death. So Cockie issued the astounding statement,
"Baroness Cockie Birkbeck Blixen Hoogterp wishes it to
be known that she has not yet been screwed in her coffin."
(*SHE takes down a rifle mounted on the wall.*) The first
rifle Bror ever gave me—with a telescopic sight. My old
Somali gunbearer called it, "Lioness Blixen's Christian
weapon." (*To Ismael.*) What do you mean, Ismael? (*As
Ismael.*) I mean, Memsahib, the arrow is Allah's way, but
the Christian way is with bullets. (*To audience.*) I
understand that after reading my first book, Bror
commented, "*Seven Gothic Tales.* Couldn't we have done
with four?" The same old Bror. (*SHE takes aim with the
gun. As Pierrot.*)
Beware the face of Harlequin, his mouth, his eyes,
For underneath his mask, an alien visage lies.

(*SHE lays the gun on the desk. A FOG HORN sounds
twice. SHE pauses to listen.   AFRICAN MUSIC
underscores, with LIGHT change.*)

KAREN. (*To audience.*) When I divorced Bror in Africa,
I blessed him in my anger. I couldn't hate him. I knew
there were demons enough in my heart without adding
another. The Bror I choose to remember is young and
happy, a virile bridegroom rowing out to my ship anchored
in Kilindini Harbor at Mombasa. He climbs aboard and
takes me in his arms. We row back to shore in the

incredible heat. That night we sleep together and are married the next morning, with Prince Wilhelm of Sweden as best man. At four in the afternoon we entrain for Nairobi in the Governor's personal dining car. The wedding supper, the rattling wheels, the vistas of night, the moon and Venus, the dark plains and the gold of morning all spent with Bror—this is my eternal beginning.

(MUSIC out, LIGHT to normal. FOG HORN.)

KAREN. I think Triton is blowing his wreathed horn tonight. In the old days, a steamer crossed the sea regularly between Sweden and Copenhagen. When I came home from Africa for good, that sound was one of the things I looked forward to. One of the few things. What I didn't look forward to was the bourgeois life in this house. Dear God, with the spirit of Lucifer still alive in the universe and represented on every side, I allowed myself to be drawn back to a pleasant, loving, infinitely kind and meddling family milieu in amiable, most cordially tolerant Denmark.
    Aunt Bess didn't waste a minute.

(SHE pounds a shoe as if it were a gavel. LIGHT change.)

KAREN. *(As Aunt Bess.)* I've called this meeting of the family to decide Tanne's future. Lidda, you and George sit there. Thomas, take the leather chair, and Jonna, the footstool. Elle and Knud in the window seat. Aage, you and Koosje pull the two armchairs into the circle. Ingeborg! Come out of the kitchen and sit down! Family Council is now in session! The meeting will come to order! (*Banging shoe once more. To audience.*) Listen, all of you! The thought of returning to Denmark is a stone on my heart. Instead of boarding that cursed ship in Mombasa, I'd gladly have gone to China as a missionary, or sold newspapers on the streets of Liverpool. I'd even have sold myself into the white slave trade, if I'd known where to sign up. (*To Aunt Bess.*) Or perhaps I could write, Aunt Bess.

(*LIGHT to normal. Taking up the glass and toasting.*)

KAREN. (*To Father.*) To us, Father, the two prodigals. (*To audience.*) The trouble was, I went to Africa a Dane and came back a Masai. Father went to America a Dane and came back a Chippewa. (*To audience.*) Father had his own pact with Lucifer. I've never felt alone in my affliction, because it was also Father's affliction. There was no help for syphilis in his time. Yes, the aristocratic Wilhelm Dinesen hanged himself in his rooms in Copenhagen three weeks before my tenth birthday. Aunt Lidda broke the news to us. "Your father is dead," she whispered softly, apologetically. I couldn't stop shaking. Ea ran to fetch Mother. "Tanne is trembling so," she said. But I wasn't going to speak of my father's death. Perhaps it's the champagne. Abstinence, yes, Dr. Ziersen.

I was in Africa for seventeen years, that wild and unforgettable domain. But they were hard times. I had no more money and could not make the farm pay. It was too high up for growing coffee. When I knew I was losing the farm, Farah was with me to the end. On those humiliating trips to Nairobi with such sorry aims as keeping my

creditors quiet or bargaining for a better price on the farm
or begging the Government for a piece of land in the
Reserve for the natives—Farah was there.

*(AFRICAN SOUNDS fade in again, with a flute obligato.
LIGHT change to gold.)*

KAREN. For these expeditions of beggary, he unlocked
chests I'd never seen before. He brought out silk robes,
gold-embroidered waistcoats and turbans in glowing and
burning reds and blues, or all white, which is a rare thing
to see and must be the gala head-dress of the Somali.
Dressed in these, he looked like a caliph's bodyguard. He
followed me, very erect, at a distance of five feet, as I
walked up and down Nairobi streets in my old slacks and
patched shoes. One day, a white man, scruffy and derelict,
snarled at Farah, "Get off the sidewalk, you damn nigger!"

*(LIGHT and SOUND cues out. SHE removes and folds the
shawl.)*

KAREN. The superiority of the white race is such an
illusion. The Somalis have it all over us. They're dignified
and proud and afraid of nothing. They go straight for
lions—which recognize them and are afraid of Somalis.
Once a man at Swedo died of plague, and all except the
Somalis ran away. *(To Farah.)* Farah, aren't you afraid of
infection? *(As Farah, shrugging.)* No, Memsahib. If it is
Allah's will that I die, I die. If Allah wishes me to live, I
live. Allah's will be done. *(To audience.)* Farah and I
became a true Unity.

I left Africa in 1931. When I bade farewell to the farm, I knew that wherever I might be in the future, I'd always wonder if there was rain at Ngong. When the S.S. Mantola left the quay at Mombasa, I watched Farah's dark immovable figure grow smaller and at last disappear. (*To Farah.*) Farah, my friend by the grace of God! We were a Unity, you and I. Even the same age. Now you're dead— some fifteen years. I remember how, whenever I returned to the farm after being away, you'd greet me ... (*As Farah.*) I see you, Memsahib. (*To Farah.*) I see you, Farah.

(SHE sits on the chest. LIGHT change to gold.)

KAREN. I see you in a thousand different ways. I see you at Nakura, when my great deerhound Dusk ran away into the darkness and was lost. I searched three days, but couldn't find him. I cried, because I had to go back to the farm. So you came to Nakura to search for Dusk. You got a mule and rode into the mountains. There were leopards in the hills, and many dangers. But on a Sunday morning you found him. He was lying beside a dead zebra foal. Dusk was hurt in the chest by a kick. He was coughing blood. He whined when he saw you, and his tail moved.

(AFRICAN MUSIC underscores.)

KAREN. You carried him back to Nakura, that cursed place. He died in your arms that same afternoon. You'd never had a feeling for any dog. It isn't the Mohammedan way. But you cried for Dusk, because I loved him. You were crying for me, Farah. Everything you did or felt was for me. No friend, brother or lover has ever done for me what you did. When my ship left Mombasa, our eyes were locked on each other. My breath was gone. Did you feel it, too? The Unity—broken?

(MUSIC out, LIGHT to normal.)

KAREN. *(To audience.)* When we docked in Marseilles, Tommy was there to meet me. "Good Lord, Tanne," he said, "you look like a wraith." Well, I did. My stockings were hanging in eels around my ankles. And I had a hole in my sweater. *(Standing. To Thomas.)* Damn it, Tommy, get me to a corsetière. I need a pair of garters tout de suite. Then on to the Clinique at Montreux for treatment of my scandalous infirmity. Then I want to ride a motor scooter through the streets of Paris. And I wonder if you'll give me enough money to live for two years, while I learn how to write? *(Pause.)* You will? Oh, Tommy, I promise to buy no new clothes, and I can easily live on bread and water, though I can't live without fun. Would it cost much to live in Rome? I love Rome. I—*(Crestfallen.)* Denmark? Rungstedlund? *(SHE goes to the book shelf and takes down "Seven Gothic Tales." To audience.)* Tommy staked me to *Seven Gothic Tales.* It was "Book-of-the-Month" in America. When the news came, the family was elated. Aunt Bess crowed, "Your first book, Tanne! Wait till your father's sisters hear about this!" *(SHE finds her jewelry box.)* My jewelry. I forgot to select jewelry for the trip. *(SHE reclines on the cushions beside the armoire and sorts through the jewelry.)* I'll take my pearls. And the lapis pin. The cameo. My beautiful garnets, yes. And this. I love delicate jewelry. (*Holding up beads.*) These amber beads were given to me by Farah. They are the color of Africa. I'm never without them. (*Putting them on.*) I used to think there were three cures for unhappiness: suicide, America and the Foreign Legion. Now I know there's a fourth. Publication. Oh, I still have periods of depression, even with my literary success. I tried suicide years ago and failed. Now I'm trying America. If that doesn't make me happy, there's still the Foreign Legion. All those surly, sinewy, sun-burned soldiers. (*Drolly.*) If they don't make me happy—and I don't see why they shouldn't—I can always try suicide again. (*SHE gets up stiffly and heads for the gramophone on stage left.*) But I'm too old for suicide. Besides, it would be déclassé. And I would prefer the Foreign Legion. (*SHE starts the gramophone.*)

RECORDED VOICE & KAREN. (*Singing.*)
You know what happened to Cinderella,
She lost her slipper and found a fella,
You know, honest and true,
Brown eyes should never be blue.

(*In an unsteady, rickety fashion, SHE attempts to dance. To audience.*)

KAREN. These days I dance better than I walk.

(*As SHE sways dreamily with the music, we see her lips form the words, "Oh, Denys."*)

RECORDED VOICE & KAREN. (*Singing.*)
Brown eyes, look up and smile,

Smiling is always in style.
Tears only add to your blues and troubles,
Troubles will float away just like bubbles.
You know, honest and true,
Brown eyes should never be blue.

(The song continues to end of act. The cuckoo CLOCK now begins to count midnight.)

KAREN. *(To clock.)* Kikuyu cuckoo. *(To Clara.)* Clara! The New Year is coming in!

(The SOUNDS of celebration, FIRECRACKERS and a CAR HORN begin. FIREWORKS flash at the window. SHE throws the cape over her shoulders.)

KAREN. *(To audience.)* If only my rifle were loaded, I'd fire a Christian bullet toward Sweden, to tell the world I'm going to America! *(To Clara.)* Clara! The fireworks are beginning! I'll watch from the veranda! *(To audience.)* Happy New Year!

(SHE exits through upstage door, ringing the bell. Stage BLACK.)

END OF ACT I

ACT II

AT RISE: We hear the GRAMOPHONE playing Handel's "Where'er You Walk." LIGHTS up on Karen's rooms. Long lace curtains now hang at the windows. It is a spring night after Karen's return from America. The room is uncluttered and simple. The upstage door to the veranda is open, though a screen door is shut. KAREN sits on a basket seat beside the gramophone at stage left. SHE is dressed in loose trousers and a turtleneck sweater. SHE wears the amber beads. At her feet are a framed picture of Denys, a flashlight, typewritten pages and the ice bucket containing champagne. SHE leans on a cane, sipping champagne. The porcelain vases hold flowers. The Somali shawl hangs on the back of her desk chair. Blueprints lean against the desk. The burgundy cape hangs on the corner of the screen. A portrait, yet unseen, leans against the back of the armoire. On the bottom shelf of the small table, a glass and beaker of water are placed.

RECORDED VOICE & KAREN. (*Singing.*)
Where'er you walk
Cool gales shall fan the glade,
Trees where you sit
Shall crowd into a shade.

*(KAREN removes the needle from the record and turns off
the gramophone. SHE picks up a paper from the floor
and shines a FLASHLIGHT on it to read more easily.)*

KAREN. *(To audience.)* Page fourteen. I'm writing a
sequel to my book, *Out of Africa.* There's little time left to
me now. I know that. I was born in this house and I'll die
in it. So I must finish this in order to close the parenthesis
of my life with a flourish. The seed for it came to me on
my return flight from America. I'm calling it *Shadows on
the Grass. (Reading.)* "When I sold all the contents of my
house in Africa, the panelled rooms became sounding
boards. If I sat down on one of the packing cases
containing things to be sent off, voices and tunes of old
rang through the nobly bare room intensified, clear." *(To
audience.)* To write this requires something beyond
possibility—that I return to Africa. "Baroness, it cannot
be," Dr. Ziersen says. And this time the old fogey is right.
He knows that in New York, I ended up in Harkness
Pavilion, with I.V.'s providing glucose and new blood.
Drip, drip, drip. It was stupefyingly dull. With New York
at my feet, I was immobile in that sterile setting.
(Standing.) "Anorexia," the doctor said. I could have told
him that. I finally couldn't keep up with the electrifying
pace of New York. *(To Clara, calling.)* Clara! You go on
to bed. I'm going to stay up awhile. I'm still on New York
time. *(Crossing to desk with cane, which SHE places on
the desk. To audience.)* Three months of dinner parties,
excitement and reckless infatuation with the American
public. Ah, New York. I've fallen in love with that unholy
place. *(SHE finds a map of New York City, and puts on*

her glasses.) I went everywhere. Here. The beautiful Empire State Building. The Brooklyn Bridge. I crossed here on the Staten Island Ferry and saw the Statue of Liberty. This is Central Park. And everywhere are pigeons. We have pigeons in Denmark, but the ones in New York are different—they cough. (*SHE takes off glasses.*) I worship the demon that possesses New York. I don't think I'll ever fall in love with anything that is demon-free. To come back here is more than I can bear. (*SHE takes the burgundy cape from the screen.*) Tove mended the Cape of Good Hope and returned it today. She ripped it, clambering out of a taxi at the Metropolitan Opera to find her escort. It was the premiere of Samuel Barber's *Vanessa.* That night I wore Sappho with Iphigenie and Max. Mr. Barber arranged for Gian Carlo Menotti to be Tove's escort. In America, it's called a "blind date." Well, of course, Tove was nervous. Who wouldn't be? Italian men can be so exciting.

Since then, Tove has talked about "Gian Carlo" incessantly. She did again today. "Gian Carlo said this, Gian Carlo said that." And with that mooning, schoolgirl look in her eyes, so inappropriate for a seventy-four-year-old. (*SHE drapes the cape over the desk chair.*) The first day I sat for my portrait in New York, Tove fidgeted so—the artist suggested she wait in a nearby restaurant called "The Stage Delicatessen." That was a mistake. Tove discovered something almost as exciting as Italian men. Cheese blintzes. (*SHE brings out the portrait from behind the armoire.*) The artist was most agreeable. His name is Mr. Calvin. He said he loved painting me. This will go to a Danish collection. (*SHE turns the portrait toward the audience. It is a picture of herself in the Pierrot costume.*)

Well? (*Pause.*) This looks as if I'm smiling. Actually I was grinding my teeth, because Mr. Calvin wouldn't let me talk. I wanted to tell him one of my stories, but he told me to be still. (*SHE takes it to the basket seat at stage left, where SHE leans it against the armoire door. SHE sits down.*) The nose is very nice. I asked Mr. Calvin to make it beautiful. I consider my nose a minor misfortune that in the course of time has become part of me. Not that it ever preyed on my mind, but as long as his brush was available, why not correct Mother Nature's astigmatism?

KAREN. (*To Pierrot in the painting.*)
Ah, Pierrot, how fey you are,
How piquant, sportive, gay you are.

(*To audience.*) Alas, New York offered up no masquerade ball for Pierrot. (*To Dr. Ziersen.*) Only one little glass, Dr. Ziersen. (*As Dr. Ziersen, slowly.*) Baroness, you are a bad girl. You are disregarding my instructions. Abstinence. Abstinence is our watchword. (*To Dr. Ziersen.*) Your watchword, Doctor, not mine. (*SHE pours herself a glass of champagne. To audience.*) Dr. Ziersen is concerned for my weight loss. I don't mind being gaunt. But I do mind being ordered about. I always knew I mustn't be fat. I felt it preferable to suffer the pangs of hunger. Being overweight cramped my style. If you want to get thin, I can help you. Try Marienbad pills, a laxative you take with every meal. Years ago, I took them all the time. Of course, my Nemesis finally obviated that need. (*Looking at portrait.*) Mr. Calvin has captured my eyes admirably. He was surprised when I told him I use belladonna in them. It makes them sparkle. That little poison is Egyptian beauty secret number four.

I suppose you think this portrait shows me handsomer than I am. Yes, you do. I can hear you thinking. (*Studying portrait.*) I believe it makes me look distingué. People do not look distinguished in person. Distinguished is for portraits. (*SHE stands and carries the picture to the end table, where SHE leans it against the side of the armoire. To portrait.*)
No carnival for you, Pierrot,
No bright Manhattan masquerade,
No dancing cavalcade,
No wild parade.

(*To audience.*) But that doesn't matter. In America, I was in a warm, welcoming spotlight for the first time in my life. I crave listening ears. I crave them with a passion. Listen, world, to my fantastic tales!

(*SHE takes a page from the desk. MUSIC of Africa underscores. LIGHT change.*)

KAREN. (*Reading aloud.*) "When, one day, I rode out on the farm and through the forest, which was still fresh after the short rains, I came upon a place of disaster. A young Kikuyu, whose name was Kitau, had not managed to get away quickly enough when a big tree fell. His fellow-workers had dragged him out and laid him on the grass. He was lying in a pool of blood, his leg smashed above the knee and sticking out from his body at a grotesque and cruel angle.

"I had the Natives hold my horse and sent off a runner to fetch Farah with the car, so that I might drive Kitau to the hospital in Nairobi. Meanwhile, Kitau was in great

pain, weeping all the time. 'Saidea mimi'—help me—
'Msabu,' he wailed. Long spasms of pain ran through his
body.

"In my distress, I put my hand into the pocket of my
old khaki slacks, and felt a letter which I had just received
from King Christian X of Denmark. It was a kind
expression of gratitude for a lion skin which I had sent
him.

" 'I have got something, Kitau, something mzuri
sana—very excellent, indeed. I have got a Barua a
Soldani—a letter from a king, in his own hand. And that is
a thing which all people know will do away with pain,
however bad.'

"At that, I laid the King's letter on his chest and my
hand upon it. I endeavored, I believe—out there in the
forest, where Kitau and I were as if alone—to lay the whole
of my strength into it. Almost at once, my words and
gesture sent an effect through him. His distorted face
smoothed out and he closed his eyes. After a while, he
again looked up at me. 'Yes, Msabu, it is very excellent,
indeed. Keep the Barua a Soldani against me, or the bad
pain will come back.'

"At last Farah arrived. All the way into Nairobi, I held
the King's letter in position. They set his broken leg at the
hospital. When Kitau got out, he could walk, though with
a limp. Amongst my stock of medicine, the Barua a
Soldani occupied a place of its own. The Natives asked for
its miracle-working powers over and over again. No ache or
pain could hold out against it. I finally had a leather bag
with a string made for it. I have still got the King's letter,

but it is now undecipherable, brown and stiff with blood of long ago."

(*MUSIC out, LIGHT to normal.*)

KAREN. (*To audience.*) America listened to me. It was the love affair of my life. I'm better understood and accepted there. In my *Anecdotes of Destiny* was a story which a Danish critic called pornography. (*To critic.*) Pornography? A harmless liaison between a man and an angel? Really, Mr. Nielsen, you do presume. (*Sitting at desk. To audience.*) If Mr. Nielsen had his way, he would decide for everyone what is art and what isn't. And—as is often the case with such men—he is uncultured, though full of religious pretension.

There's something in the Danish mentality I can't take. The Danes speak all the time about their sense of humor. Det danske lune. But they're humorless. It's an odd feeling to be the only intoxicated one at a party of sober Danes. And I mean sober. (*SHE drapes the Somali shawl around her shoulders.*) There's a chill in the air tonight. Here at Rungstedlund, we simply pile on more clothing. The Americans are far ahead of us in heating. It's so controlled and even. It was harsh winter in New York, yet my suite at the Cosmopolitan Club was entirely comfortable. I know I can't endure another winter here on the coast. (*SHE briefly unrolls the set of blueprints.*) So I have a plan. Here. Steen Eiler Rasmussen has drawn up these blueprints. He's Rungsted's leading architect. The Professor will modernize the house with central heating and plumbing. He was shocked when he learned there were no toilets in the house.

(*To Professor.*) It is 1959, Professor, and time for this medieval household to march bravely though belatedly into the twentieth century. (*SHE picks up the chamber pot. To audience.*) No more reminders of the primitive past. The hour for modernization has struck!

(*The Cuckoo CLOCK sounds the half hour.*)

KAREN. Away with chamber pots! Just think—doing it all under one roof. If Aunt Bess were alive, she'd have none of it. (*To Aunt Bess.*) But, Aunt Bess, Tommy and Jonna have plumbing. Anders has it. Why, Father's sisters all had plumbing—(*As Aunt Bess.*) Oh, your father's sisters! Wouldn't they just put in plumbing, with their high and mighty airs? They always thought they were too good for our traditional Danish ways. (*Holding the pot aloft.*) Just look at this beautiful thing, Tanne. Royal Copenhagen. It's part of our history. Why, your Grandmother Westenholz sat on it, God rest her soul. (*Examining the rim.*) This crack mysteriously appeared the night she died in 1915. It was like an omen. Poor little Moonbeam. (*To audience.*) My nephews call this "Moonbeam's Thunder Mug." (*Crossing to stage left.*) It will look lovely planted with African violets. I wonder why they're called African? I never saw one violet in Kenya. (*SHE dumps the ice into the pot.*) Champagne for everyone! (*Sitting on basket seat.*) Mother wanted plumbing in the house for years, but Aunt Bess talked her out of it each time. Mother came to Africa twice, once in 1924 and again in 1927. During both visits, she proclaimed Mbogani House more up-to-date than Rungstedlund.

She was right. Mbogani was more everything than Rungstedlund. A sprawling fieldstone manor with marvelous plumbing, stone mantels, fine paneling with paved terrace, green lawn and dark forest beyond. The day I left the farm for good, I had tea on the millstone table on the terrace outside. There was a floating mist in the creeks. It was a cool morning, and to the West, the Ngong Hills lived gravely through another moment of their many thousand years. I felt cold, as if I'd been up there. Where's my scarf? (*SHE finds the scarf in the armoire drawer and wraps it about her neck.*) I think it grew another foot in New York.

(African MUSIC underscores.)

KAREN. I was at the millstone table the afternoon the stork appeared. I looked up and there it was, standing on the lawn. A European stork. Farah said it was a wandering caliph from *A Thousand and One Nights*, using the clever disguise of a bird. One wing was broken and Farah fixed it. The bird's diet of frogs kept Farah busy. The stork took to walking through the house. When he came to my bedroom, he fought duels with his image in the looking-glass. Such swaggering and flapping of wings. He looked as if he flew out of a fairy tale by Hans Christian Andersen.

(MUSIC out.)

KAREN. When we were children, Father told us a parable about a stork. He told it so often, we knew it by heart. May I show you? (*SHE stands and opens one of the armoire doors. With a lipstick, SHE sets about drawing a stork on the mirror.*) In a little round house with a round window and a little triangular garden in front, there lived a man. Not far from the house there was a pond with fish in it.

One night the man was awakened by a terrible noise, and set out in the dark to find the cause. He took the road to the pond. He first ran to the South. Here he stumbled over a big stone in the middle of the road, and a little farther he fell into a ditch, got up, fell into a ditch, got up, fell into a third ditch, and got out of that.

Then he realized he had been mistaken, and ran back to the North. But here again the noise seemed to come from the South, and he again ran back there. He first stumbled over a big stone in the middle of the road, then a little later he fell into a ditch, got up, fell into another ditch, got up, fell into a third ditch, and got out of that. He now distinctly heard the noise come from the end of the pond. He rushed to the place, and saw a big leakage in the dam, and the water running out with all the fish in it. He set to work and stopped the hole, and only when this had been done did he go back to bed.

When now the next morning the man looked out of his little round window, what did he see? A stork.

"Look for the stork," Father said. "In every trial, hold to your purpose. Keep the faith and you'll see the stork."

The tight place, the dark pit in which I've lain—was it the stork's talon? The despair and pain—was it the

rapacious beak? What will come out of it? Are we all
perfecting—each of us—a microcosm? I know that my
greatest moments in life were those in which I glimpsed
the stork. I wonder, when the design of my life is
completed, shall I, shall others, see the stork? (*SHE sits
down and takes another sip.*) Too many glasses of this, Dr.
Ziersen, and I'll be seeing goldfish. (*SHE harks to a noise
and gets up.*) Did you hear that? I wonder if she's angry
with me? (*Calling to Clara.*) Clara, did you slam your
door? (*To audience.*) Clara thinks I'm autocratic, which, of
course, isn't true. She also thinks I'm devious. Ridiculous.
(*Finding a letter on the small table beside the armoire.
Calling to Clara.*) Clara? About this invitation to the
Librarians' Association in Copenhagen: I want you to send
them a letter tomorrow saying I'll be happy to address
them on August 15th. Then call them on August 14th and
cancel. (*SHE winces in pain. To audience.*) Excuse me.
(*SHE lies on the floor and pulls up her knees.*) This is the
only position that relieves the pain of a syphilitic spine.
When I had my last operation, a doctor in Copenhagen
said, "Tanne Blixen is very clever, but the cleverest thing
she's ever done is to survive." It hasn't been cleverness.
I've been like Jacob raging at Fate, wrestling with the
angel at Peniel. (*Shouting.*) I will not let thee go, except
thou bless me!

(*LIGHT change as SHE slowly sits up.*)

KAREN. Or is my pain the revenge of the Beast? If so,
then I confess my sin—I betrayed Lucifer and was at home
with the angels in Heaven for a little while. Ecstasy and

desire came to me at Mbogani House. Oh, Denys, for a
moment you made me forget the awful, the inescapable
truth—that God had cast me from Heaven.

(SHE is fully sitting up. MUSIC fades in.)

KAREN. To be afflicted with a fatal sexual disease
binds one to an unseen brotherhood, both living and dead.
Link by link, a chain is forged—of parents, sisters,
brothers, of friends and lovers, of Samaritans and cure-
seekers. It is a timeless communion of saints that gathers
itself around one, a compassionate brotherhood beyond
moral judgment.
I have always believed that life demands of us that we
love it, not merely certain sides of it and not only one's
own ideas and ideals, but life itself in all its forms, before
it will give us anything in return. I could not, therefore,
see myself for long in any tragic light. All my life, I have
joyfully clung to the dark angel. *(Crying out.)* I will not
let thee go, except thou bless me!

*(MUSIC out, LIGHT to normal. The call of a SEAGULL
is heard.)*

KAREN. Hear that? I'm hovering like that seagull. The
world is happy and splendid, but I feel I'm not a part of it.
I hover over life, waiting to die. I don't mean to sound
morbid, because I believe it's a great and lovely experience
to die. I've even chosen my burial site. Under a beech tree
at the foot of the hill, close to the grave of my darling dog,
Pasop. A German Shepherd. Did I say German? I mean,

Alsatian. Since the Nazi occupation of Denmark, we Danes don't say the word "German" anymore. This house was a way station for Jews escaping by boat to Sweden. I had Nazis in the parlor and Jews in the pantry. (*SHE begins the process of standing up.*) These days, I simply don't have enough strength. Oh, I've had blood transfusions to strengthen me, but they haven't. All because last year, the doctors removed a good part of my stomach. I should've told them to remove only the bad part. (*SHE stands feebly, relieved of pain.*) Cessation of pain is one of the great joys of life. It gives one reprieve from the Underworld. Well, all sorrows can be borne, if you put them into a story. The divine art is the story. In the beginning was the story. *(At the desk, glasses on, alternately typing and speaking.)* When I wrote *Winter's Tales*, I began with a flavor of each tale, a tingle. Then I found the characters, and they took over. They made the design. I simply permitted them their liberty. I wrote about the characters within the design. For other writers, this seems an unnatural thing, but a proper tale has a shape, an outline.

In a painting, even the frame is important. Where does the picture end? Where does the line go that cuts off the picture? (*Taking off glasses, SHE calls attention to a small painting, her own.*) I was a painter before I was a writer. There's one face in New York I should like to have painted. Marilyn Monroe's. I met her as I had hoped. She had just completed a movie with a very strange title. (*SHE checks her journal.*) I've written it down in my journal. Oh, here. *Some Like It Hot.*

Miss Monroe and Arthur Miller called for me in their car and took me to luncheon at the home of Carson

McCullers, another playwright. Miss Monroe wore a clinging sheath dress of black satin, with a dramatically deep decolletage. I wore Sober Truth, with Tristan and Isolde.

It isn't that Miss Monroe is pretty, although of course she's incredibly pretty—but that she radiates at the same time unbounded vitality and a kind of unbelievable innocence. I've met the same in a lion cub that my native servants in Africa brought to me. I wouldn't keep it.

Before the afternoon ended, Mrs. McCullers put a record on the gramophone, and we danced, Miss Monroe and I.

(Slow BLUES underscores, as KAREN stands, stretching her arms across the desk, as if grasping Marilyn's hands. To Marilyn, tenderly.)

Du bist wie eine Blume,
So hold und schön und rein.
Child, you are like a flower,
So pure and sweet and fair,
It wrings my heart with anguish.

KAREN. (*To audience.*) I tried to share my Egyptian beauty secrets with her, but she didn't seem interested.

(MUSIC out. Tottering back into chair.)

KAREN. The terra firma doesn't feel so firma.

It must be a burden for that poor girl to have the world's adulation. I've always found it intolerable being a love object. Perhaps this attitude is the difference between

Miss Monroe and myself. This, and whatever else lies
between Sober Truth and *Some Like It Hot*. *(SHE finds a
letter in a stack of correspondence.)* Clara will be busy
tomorrow. But this I'll answer myself. It's from my chef
in Africa, Kamante Gatura.

(African MUSIC underscores.)

   KAREN. *(Reading aloud.)*
   "To honored Mrs. Karen from your good and faithful
servant Kamante, I pray that God will be kind to you now
and then. I like to come to Denmark to take service with
you once more, but I think Kamante be too old." *(To
audience.)* He was nine when I first met him, his legs thin
as sticks and covered with deep sores. I took him to the
Scotland Mission near the Kikuyu Station, and the brothers
cured him. *(Reading aloud.)*
   "Mrs. Karen, I was not forget you. If we was bird, we
fly and see you. Then we turn. Write and tell us if you
turn. We think you turn. Because why? We think that you
shall never can forget us." *(To audience.)* Where the great
chef walks in deep thought, full of knowledge, nobody sees
anything but a little bandy-legged Kikuyu with a flat, still
face. *(SHE briefly returns to typing. As Kamante.)* Mrs.
Karen, I do not believe that you can write a book. *(To
audience.)* That is is what Kamante said one day at
Mbogani House. He had stood by the wall for hours,
watching me at the typewriter. *(To Kamante.)* And why
not, Kamante? *(SHE goes to the shelves and picks out a
large blue book. As Kamante.)* Look, Mrs. Karen, this is a
good book. *(To Kamante.)* Of course. It is *The Odyssey* by

Homer. (*Dangling it by the cover. As Kamante.*) But it hangs together from the one end to the other. Even if you hold it up and shake it strongly, it does not come to pieces. This Bwana Homer who has written it is very clever. But what you write is some here and some there. When the people forget to close the door, it blows about, even down on the floor. No, it will not be a good book, I think. And I do not believe that your book can be made blue like Bwana Homer's book. (*To Kamante, laughing.*) Oh, Kamante.

(*MUSIC out.*)

KAREN. (*To audience.*) So there he stood, the great chef, looking very solemn and separate. I think he was aware of his separateness, with the arrogant greatness of soul of the dwarf, who, when he finds himself at odds with the world, holds the world to be crooked.

(*WE hear the distant sound of a TRAIN WHISTLE.*)

KAREN. A sound from childhood. (*To Elle.*) Elle! Listen! (*SHE opens the window behind the desk. To audience.*) We would dream of all the famous train trips we'd make together. The Trans-Siberian route, the Great Northern across America ...

(*The WHISTLE trails away.*)

KAREN. Elle died while I was in Boston. The telegram was waiting when I returned to New York. (*Whispering to herself.*) Be still, my soul. (*To audience.*) "Das Schloss am

Meer." It is what we called this place, Elle and I. The
Castle by the Sea. When the winter gales blew and the
waves crashed on the rocks, we were sisters of Fate in our
citadel.
Now the wind and waves together
Share a melancholy sleep,
And a song of mourning rises
From the castle where I weep.

*(SHE sits on the chest at downstage left and lights a
     cigarette, using a holder.)*

KAREN. I have learned to live with loneliness. Oh, I
have my coterie of devoted young men who fawn at my
feet. They want to be writers. I play the sorceress. I
promise them magic, then withhold it. It is my obsession
and my satisfaction to play this game. *(SHE peers at her
watch.)* Almost midnight. My brother Tommy is coming
to breakfast tomorrow morning. Oh, dear, what shall I
serve him? No, Tove, not your blintzes. "I'll be there at
nine," he said.
   The Swahili word for nine is "tisa." But in Danish,
"tisse" means "to pee." So when I was new in Africa, and a
shy young Scandinavian dairyman was teaching me how to
count in Swahili, he blushingly avoided nine. *(As tutor,
counting.)* Moja, mbili, tatu, nne, tano, sita, sabe, nane ...
er, excuse me, Baroness, but they have not got nine in
Swahili. *(To tutor.)* But, Mr. Nordstrum, you mean they
can only count up to eight? *(As tutor.)* Oh, no, Baroness,
they have got ten, eleven, twelve and so on. They just
don't have nine. *(To tutor.)* But how does that work? What

do they do when they come to nineteen? (*As tutor.*) They
have not got nineteen. Nor ninety, nor nine hundred. But
apart from that, they have got all the other numbers.

I know what. I'll ask Clara to prepare Tommy's
favorite. Broiled mushrooms on rounds of toast. She cooks
them to perfection. "Mushrooms for breakfast?" he'll say.
"My sister is getting crazier every day." That well may be.
I wish people would treat me like a lunatic. It would
simplify everything.

Tommy didn't marry until he was thirty-three. I don't
know what took him so long, unless he was waiting for
Jonna, a red-haired girl with black eyes who could swim
underwater and play the cello. Not at the same time.
(*Referring to the cushions by her feet.*) These are from
Mbogani House. I've had them recovered three times.
Denys called this "Scheherazade's Place." Here I would sit
by firelight and tell him my stories. (*SHE briefly draws the
edge of the black fascinator over her lower face.*) He was
the Sultan and I was Scheherazade.

Denys Finch Hatton had a trait of character which to me
was very precious. He liked to hear a story told. This
Oxford classicist who read both Greek and Latin was like
the Natives of Africa, who can't read.

If you say to them, "Once there was a man who had an
elephant with two heads," you have got them all with you.
"But, Memsahib," they gasp, "how did this man manage to
feed an elephant with two heads?" Denys was like that.
Childlike.

Every time he came to the farm, he'd ask, "Have you
got a story?"

Yes, I have a story.

(LIGHTS dim. SPOT only on KAREN.)

KAREN. An old Danish shipowner sat and thought of his young days and of how, when he was sixteen years old, he had spent a night in a brothel in Singapore. He had come with the sailors of his father's ship, and had sat and talked with an old Chinese woman. When she heard he was a native of a distant country, she brought out her old parrot. Long, long ago, she told him, the parrot had been given her by a high-born English lover of her youth. The boy thought the bird must then be a hundred years old. It could say various sentences in the languages of all the world, picked up in the cosmopolitan atmosphere of the house. But one phrase the old China-woman's lover had taught it before he sent it to her, and that she did not understand, neither had any visitor ever been able to tell her what it meant. For many years she had given up asking. But if the boy came from far away, perhaps it was his language, and he could interpret the phrase to her. The boy was deeply, strangely moved at the suggestion. When the Chinese woman made the parrot speak its sentence, it turned out to be classic Greek. The bird spoke the words very slowly, and the boy knew enough Greek to recognize it. It was a verse from Sappho:
"The moon has sunk and the Pleiads,
And midnight is gone,
And the hours are passing, passing,
And I lie alone."

The old woman, when he translated the lines to her, smacked her lips and rolled her small slanting eyes. She asked him to say it again, and nodded her head.

(LIGHTS up. SHE looks across the stage into the armoire mirror.)

KAREN. Lioness Blixen is now old and sick. See her there. She looks like the most horrid old witch. There she sits on this Danish spring night, listening to the lapping of waves from the Sound. And yet, when I close my eyes, only Africa is real. I'm back again on the veranda at Mbogani House, waiting for my high-born English lover to return from yet another safari. *(To Denys, entreatingly.)* I missed you, Denys. Did you miss me? *(To audience.)* "Tania," he said, "there's no time on safari for missing anyone. But I did think of you happily many times." *(To Denys, imploringly.)* Happily? Happily? Don't you know you're the only person who means anything to me? My entire existence revolves around you. Denys, please, I want certainty. I want you to want certainty. *(As Denys.)* Tania, I don't want to be possessed. I want no attachments. I told you that at the outset. *(To Denys, bitterly.)* Oh, you want attachments, all right. What you don't want is their responsibilities. You fly about Africa in your Gypsy Moth. You're Peter Pan—you've literally had no home except mine. You've brought all your things here. Now suddenly, it's too confining. The walls are closing in. Your precious independence is threatened by my love. Well, maybe the rumors are true. Maybe you are seeing another woman in Nairobi, a younger—*(Distraught, becoming*

hysterical.) No, I don't believe that. I can't believe it. Is it
true, Denys? No, no, don't tell me. Oh, dear God, I don't
know what I'm saying. It's just that you're here for a
fortnight, then off for two months, back for six weeks,
gone for five months. I can't go on this way. (*Sobbing.*)
Oh, Finch Hatton, what is happening to us?

(*To herself.*)

Now all is done that could be done.

And all is done in vain.

(*To audience.*) And so, the loss of my lover and the loss
of my farm drew inexorably closer. I couldn't believe it
was happening. It was like the black cloud of grasshoppers
that appeared one day on the horizon.

(*A clicking NOISE is heard, distant, threatening. In her
imagination, she is suddenly there.*)

KAREN. Those can't be grasshoppers. That's a shadow
on the northern horizon, nothing more—a long stretch of
smoke, a town burning, but not grasshoppers.

(*Whirring, clicking SOUNDS of the swarming pestilence
grow louder.*)

KAREN. And still it comes—the cloud, the smoke—
no, neither cloud nor smoke, but something alive,
descending on us like a blizzard, whistling and shrieking
like a strong wind, little hard furious wings to all sides of
you and over your head, shining like thin blades of steel in
the sun.

(SHE flails the air with her fascinator, screaming. The SOUND builds in volume. SHE runs to the window and slams it shut. The SOUNDS stop. Distraught, SHE fumbles in the desk drawer.)

KAREN. Where are my pills? *(To Clara, screaming.)* Clara, where are my pills? *(Finding the bottle of pills, SHE slams the drawer. To audience.)* With these I transcend my fragile self, my resentments, my ancient sorrows. *(To portrait, whimpering.)* Oh, Pierrot, will you ever see the stork? *(SHE pours a glass of water from a beaker on the small table, but leaves it and reclines on the cushions by the armoire. To audience.)* I have another story. There once was a woman who had lost much—her farm, her lover. The farm was irretrievable, auctioned away to strangers. But her lover—ah, her lover—perhaps he would see the light and come back to her. With this dream in her heart, she drove to a nearby town to lunch with a friend. There was a deep sadness over the town. People turned from her. She drove up a long bamboo avenue to her friend's house. The luncheon guests were mortally sad. As she walked in, conversation stopped. "These people are no good to me," the woman thought. "I'll go back home. My lover could be there now, waiting to beg my forgiveness." But before she could leave, her hostess took her into a small sitting-room. "There's been an accident," she said. "Your lover's plane has crashed. Your lover is dead."

(We hear a SEAGULL's cry.)

KAREN. It is an irony of Fate that with the Unities all broken—Father, Farah, Denys, Africa itself—good things came too late. When the farm was lost, the rains came, rains we had prayed for in the past. Farah's wife brought their little baby, Saufe, to sleep in my bed. He was swaddled like a little acorn. The bed was so big, he disappeared into it. But I was comforted.
(Singing to baby.)
Den lille Ole med paraplyen
Ham kender alle småfolk i byen;
Hver lille pige, hver lille dreng
Han genner skaelmsk i sin lille seng.

(The cuckoo CLOCK begins to sound midnight.)

KAREN. Kikuyu cuckoo. *(SHE stands. To herself.)* No! I don't want to sleep. The flashlight! I want the flashlight, so I can gather mushrooms for Tommy's breakfast. *(SHE angrily hurls the bottle of pills across the room.)* It's a waste of time to sleep. *(To Clara.)* Clara! *(To audience.)* She must have the flashlight. Just when I need it!

(Beat.)

KAREN. To Denys Finch Hatton I owe what was the greatest joy of my life. I flew with him over Africa in his bright yellow Gypsy Moth. *(As Denys.)* Come on, Tania! Let's go up there and risk our entirely worthless lives! *(To audience.)* We went up almost every day that he lived with me. Many times we chased a pair of Eagles, who spent their lives in the air over Ngong. One day, when we were running side by side with them, Denys cut the engine, and as he did so, I heard the Eagle screech.

An old Kikuyu on the farm said, "You were up very high today, Msabu. I could not see you, only hear the aeroplane sing like a bee. Did you see God?" (*To Kikuyu.*) No, Ndwetti, I did not see God. (*As Kikuyu.*) Aha, then I do not know at all why you go on flying. (*To audience.*) Denys was buried in the Ngong Hills, high above the farm. Behind the grave, Farah and I raised three tall poles and nailed white cloth across them. From the farm, I could see the small white point on the green hill ... (*To Farah.*) There, Farah! There it is! I see it! (*To audience.*) By moonlight, it was a pale signal in the dark.

(MUSIC underscores. LIGHT changes to MOONLIGHT.)

KAREN.
From the candles and dumb shadows,
And the house where love had died,
I stole to the vast moonlight
And the whispering life outside.
But I found no lips of comfort,
No home in the moon's light
(I, little and lone and frightened
In the unfriendly night).
And suddenly I found you white and radiant,
Sleeping quietly,
Far out through the tides of darkness.
And I there in that great light
Was alone no more, nor fearful;

For there, in the homely night,
Was no thought else that mattered,
And nothing else was true,
But the white fire of moonlight,
And a white dream of you.

*(LIGHT to normal. MUSIC out. SHE moves to stage left
and picks up Denys's photograph. SHE carries it to the
bookshelves.)*

KAREN. Denys admired Rupert Brooke's poetry. Denys
was embarrassed about being prematurely bald and seldom
appeared hatless. I personally think bald men exude great
sexual magnetism. It's a regrettable symptom of our
inequitable society that men don't feel the same way about
bald women.

A strange thing—after I left Africa, I was told that a
lion and lioness often came to lie on Denys's grave. Lord
Nelson in Trafalgar Square has only bronze lions. *(To
Denys.)* Oh, Denys, I did see God over the Ngong Hills.
He appeared to me as an Eagle. He spoke to me with an
Eagle's voice. A paradox, really, that God should manifest
Himself to the daughter of Lucifer. *(Pausing to stare at her
portrait. To audience.)* I don't do justice to my portrait.
(Referring to the blueprints, as SHE moves to stage left.)
Professor Rasmussen will pick these up tomorrow. I think
I'll ask him to put in a west window for the afternoon sun.
I don't relish the upheaval the work will cause, but the
thought of no more freezing stairways and icy floors is
inducement enough. I only wish my dear mother could
have known the luxury of warmth and convenience before

she died. She left us one night in January years ago, in a
white winter. (*SHE sits in the armoire.*) I kept vigil at her
bedside. Remorse and guilt were mine, because I'd taken
her so for granted all those years, ridiculed her patriotically-
minded home, her rows of hyacinths, her tea and toast, and
all that transpired in these pleasant backwaters. (*To
Mother.*) My own Snow-white Lamb, I dreamed of you
again last night. Tommy is a little boy in a striped
sunsuit, Anders is sailing his boat on the shore, I'm in my
pinafore, running up from the forest, and you step out of
the courtyard with your red parasol. When you see me, you
put it down and hold out your arms to me. (*SHE weeps
quietly, then looks up to see the flashlight on the floor
beside the gramophone.*) Oh. The flashlight. I'm sorry,
Clara—my faithful Clara. I must be difficult to live with
sometimes. (*Pause.*) Now I can gather mushrooms. (*SHE
places a new record in the gramophone, which SHE winds.
To audience.*) I'm told that my farm in Africa has been cut
up into residential plots for Nairobi business people. The
animals have been pushed back and back, the rain forest is
fast disappearing, and poaching of white rhino and elephant
is rife.

William the Conqueror would have known what to do.
His laws forbade trespassing and poaching in his forests.
Offenders were castrated, their eyes put out and their legs
cut off. Then they were free to leave the country.

(*SHE starts the MUSIC. It is "Death and the Maiden" by
Shubert.*)

KAREN. Shubert. Such purity.

*(SHE picks up a typed page from the floor, shining the
     FLASHLIGHT on it. LIGHT change.)*

KAREN. *(Reading aloud.)* "My African existence has
sunk below the horizon. The Southern Cross for a short
while stood out after it, like a luminous track in the sky,
then faded and disappeared. What business had I ever to set
my heart on Africa?" *(Standing. To audience)* "She who
first of all sees the new moon"—that's the name the
Natives gave me. The new moon, you see, is when safari
begins. I would send Farah ahead to some unknown place
to pitch camp, and he would wait for me to follow. Still I
dream of it. A whole row of moonlit nights ahead. I'm
walking towards a lone figure waiting in the distance. He
calls out to me, "I see you, Memsahib." *(With exultation.)*
I see you, Farah.

*(SHE slowly raises the flashlight, shining it out toward the
     audience, as haunting MUSIC of Africa crossfades with
     the Shubert. A backdrop of Africa fades in and gold
     LIGHT suffuses the stage. Deep in thought, KAREN
     crosses to her desk. SHE begins typing.)*

KAREN. "If I know a song of Africa, of the Giraffe and
the African new moon lying on her back, of the ploughs in
the fields and the sweaty faces of the coffee-pickers, does
Africa know a song of me? Would the air over the plain
quiver with a color that I had worn, or the children invent a
game in which my name was, or the full moon throw a

shadow over the gravel of the drive that was like me, or would the Eagles of Ngong look out for me?"

(The AFRICAN ambiance has faded. The SHUBERT has surged back. KAREN stands and puts on her cape, takes up a basket, the flashlight and cane. To audience.)

KAREN. It's strange, but I feel so close to Paradise. Not in any religious sense, mind you. But still I feel closer to happiness and balance than I ever have. Maybe I'm seeing the stork at last. Sometimes I think I can see it. By that I mean that I believe in it. I've fallen into so many ditches, chased around the lake so many times—that I can't be sure. Still, I've received more from life than I've deserved, sign or no sign.

(LIGHT change to moonlight, as SHE moves downstage. To Denys.)

KAREN. I have answered to my fate, Denys, your family motto taken as my own: "Je responderay." *(Looking skyward.)* Is that Venus? Tommy will know if it's Venus or not. *(Facing Ngong.)* Goodnight, Denys. *(The MUSIC still playing, SHE begins exit, then pauses. To audience.)* I did see God.

(SHE exits through upstage screen door. Stage goes BLACK.)

THE END

CURTAIN ENCORE

(KAREN returns to stage with the basket full of mushrooms.)

KAREN. Your charming gift of imagination has fallen in with my own fantasies. I shall not forget you, and I beg you to remember that together we have salted sweet hours, made the years rewind, eaten all the ripened heart of life, and made a luscious pickle of the rind. Goodnight. *(At KAREN's exit, the armoire door swings open, revealing the Pierrot costume.)*

COSTUME PLOT

Pierrot costume with ruff
Plumed Pierrot hat
Plain low-heeled shoes
Long-sleeved silk blouse, high neck
Slacks (2 pairs)
White striped Somali shawl
Long knitted scarf, dark brown
Black fascinator
Fur coat (bear)
Two capes, burgundy and peacock
Gold turban
Gloves (2 pairs, lace, kid)
Wide feathered hat
Fox neck-piece
Leopard hat
Loose turtle-neck sweater
Assorted gowns, dresses & suits (about 20)
Shoes (2 pairs)

PROPERTY PLOT

FURNITURE:
Two-door armoire with mirrors
Dining table & chairs (optional)
Scandinavian porcelain stove
Bookcases
Writing table & chair
Wicker chair
Stool
End table
Farah's chest

ACCESSORIES:
Old Corona typewriter
Typewriter case
Old gramophone
Record case full of 78s
Painted Oriental screen
Rifle with telescopic sight
Oil painting of Karen as Pierrot
Large jardiniere containing spears
Oriental fan
Winter & spring curtains
Bell
Lamps
Magnifying glass
Eyeglasses
Cigarettes
Cigarette holder
Ashtray
Lighter
Mirror over end table
Bible

Blank paper
Passport
Maps of Wisconsin & New York
Magnifying glass
Journal/diary
Typed pages of manuscript
Stack of correspondence
Invitation from Librarians' Association
Pill box
Bag of toiletries: comb, blue toothbrush, tooth powder,
    glycerin soap
Makeup case: bib, powder, puff, lipstick, kohl, vial of
    belladonna
Waste basket
Champagne bucket:
    bottle of champagne,
    ice & water
Champagne flute
Worn Oriental rugs
Trunk, suitcase, hatbox
Glove case
Shoe slips
Tablecloth
Assorted books
Framed photographs
Large pillows on floor (upholstered in African fabrics)
Jewelry case: earrings, garnets, pearls, amber beads
Water carafe
China chamber pot
Scrapbook
Mandolin
Vase: dried flowers (winter) & fresh flowers (spring)
Flashlight
Basket for mushrooms

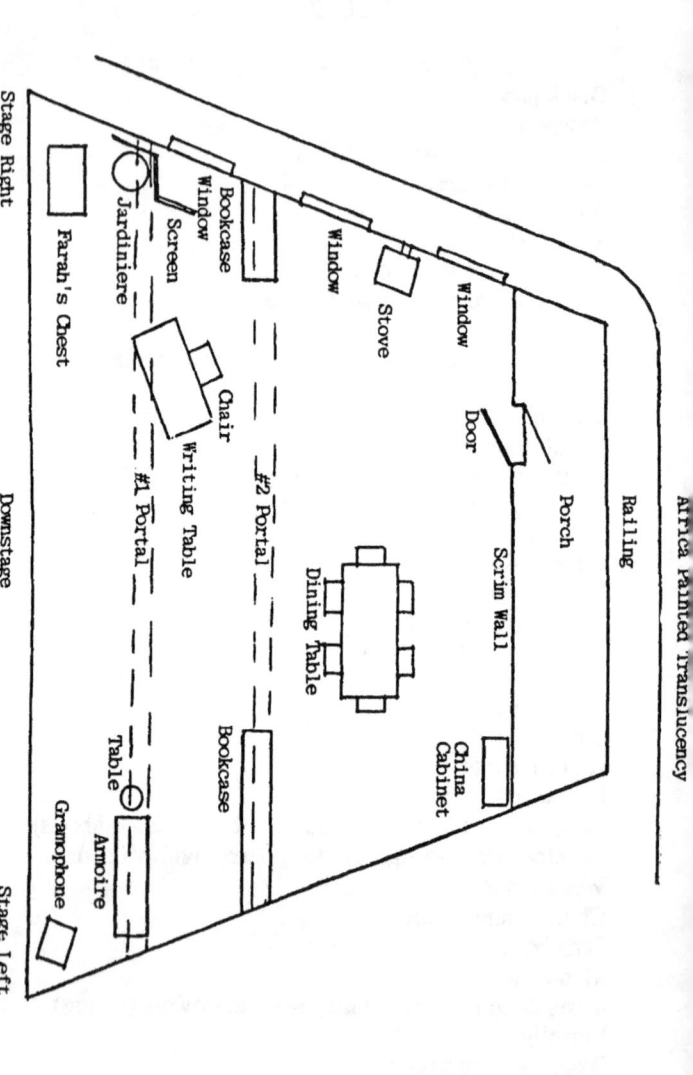

Africa Painted Translucency

Railing

Porch

Scrim Wall

China Cabinet

Dining Table

Door

Window

Stove

Window

Window

Bookcase

Screen

Jardiniere

Chair

Writing Table

Farah's Chest

#1 Portal

#2 Portal

Bookcase

Table

Amoire

Gramophone

Stage Right

Downstage

Stage Left

LUCIFER'S CHILD
Set Design by Marjorie Bradley Kellogg

DEN LILLE OLE MED PARAPLYEN

Peter Lemche

O. Jacobsen

Den lil - le   O - le med pa-ra - ply-en ham ken-der

al - le små-folk   i   by - en; hver lil - le pi - ge, hver lil-le

dreng han gen - ner skaelmsk i   sin lil - le   seng.